HOPPiNg MAD

Linda Urban

Illustrated by Henry Cole

ANDERSEN PRESS

For Claire and Jack—L. U.

For my pals Anita and Debbie,
with affection—H. C.

This paperback edition first published in 2010 by Andersen Press Ltd., 20 Vauxhall Bridge Road, London, SW1V 2SA.
First published in The United States in 2009 by Houghton Mifflin Harcourt.
Published in Australia by Random House Australia Pty., Level 3, 100 Pacific Highway, North Sydney, NSW 2060.
Text copyright © Linda Urban, 2009. Illustrations copyright © Henry Cole, 2009.
The rights of Linda Urban and Henry Cole to be identified as the author and illustrator of this work have been
asserted by them in accordance with the Copyright, Designs and Patents Act, 1988. All rights reserved.
Printed and bound in Singapore by Tien Wah Press.

10 9 8 7 6 5 4 3 2 1

British Library Cataloguing in Publication Data available. ISBN 978 1 84270 970 2

Mouse was mad. **Hopping mad.**

"You look ridiculous," said Hare.
Mouse stopped hopping.

"Let me show you how to hop properly," said Hare,
who truly was a hopping whiz.

Mouse tried to hop like Hare.
Nothing doing.

Mouse

hop-hop-flopped—

SPLISH!—

into a mucky mud puddle.

Now Mouse was really mad.
Stomping mad.

"You call that stomping?" said Bear.

Mouse stopped stomping.

"Stomping, done right, should result in the shaking of trees and the rumbling of earth," said Bear. Bear stomped.

The trees shook, the earth rumbled.

Mouse tried to stomp like Bear.

The trees did not shake.

The earth did not rumble.

Mouse

stomp-stomp-flomped—

SPLUSH!—

into another mucky mud puddle.

Now Mouse was really, really mad.
Screaming mad.

"That's hardly a scream at all," said Cat.
Mouse stopped screaming.

"When I scream, you can hear it echo through the woods."
Cat screamed to prove his point. It echoed and echoed.

Mouse opened his mouth wide and let out
the loudest scream he could manage.
No echo.

He tried arching his back like Cat

but lost his balance and fell—

SPLOSH!—

into yet another mucky mud puddle.

Now Mouse was really, really, really mad.

Rolling-around-on-the-ground mad.

"Pull your feet in," said Hedgehog.

Mouse stopped rolling.

"The best rolling is achieved when the body is a perfect sphere." Hedgehog tucked in his nose and his feet and his hands. He was a perfect sphere.

Mouse tucked in his nose and his feet and his hands.
He was not a perfect sphere, but he was close.

He pulled in his tail

and rolled around and around—

SPLOOSH!—

into the muckiest mud puddle of all.

Now Mouse was really, really, really, really mad.

Standing-still mad.

Mouse did not hop. He did not stomp.

He did not scream or roll on the ground.

He stood very, very still.

"Impressive," said Hare.
"What control," said Bear.
"Are you breathing?"
    asked Hedgehog.

Mouse took a deep breath.

He let his breath out.

Cat heard air whistle through Mouse's nose, but
he did not see Mouse move.

"Inspiring," said Cat.

Cat stood very still. He breathed deeply and tried not to move.

"Your ears twitched," said Hare.
"Let me try." But he could not keep
his tail from wiggling.

Bear tried, but when he breathed deeply, trees moved and the ground shook a little. Hedgehog came closest, but even he could not keep his bristles from bristling.

They stood together for a long time, breathing and trying to be still.

And then, Mouse realized he was no longer mad.

"I feel better now," said Mouse.

"You look better now," said Bear.

"But you need a bath," said Hedgehog.

"Good idea," said Mouse.

SPLASH!

More books you might enjoy:

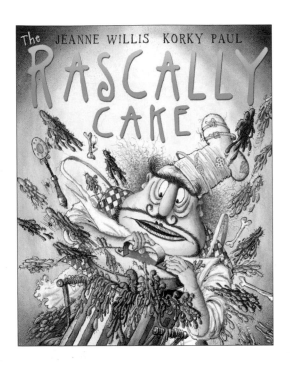